goat
kid

duck
duckling

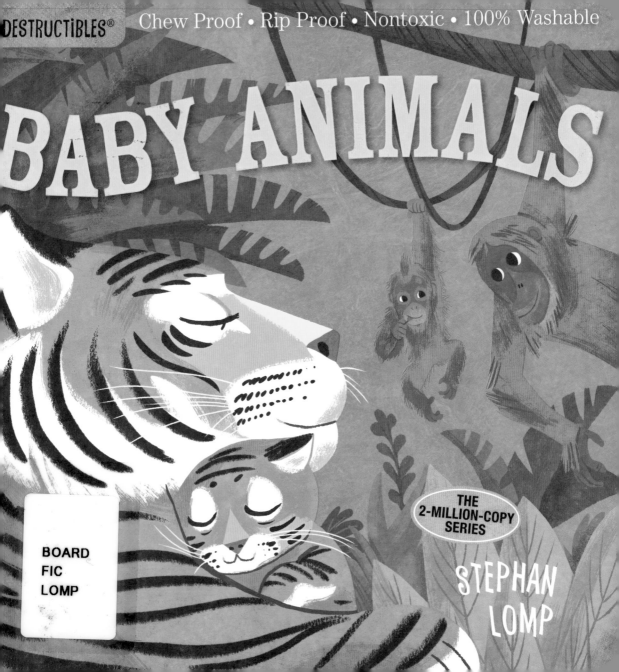

Chew Proof • Rip Proof • Nontoxic • 100% Washable

BABY ANIMALS

THE
2-MILLION-COPY
SERIES

STEPHAN
LOMP

There are all kinds of
babies in the world.

opossum
joey

sloth
cub

cat
kitten

elephant
calf

They love to eat.

monkey
infant

chipmunk
pup

koala
joey

turtle
hatchling

They love to make noise.

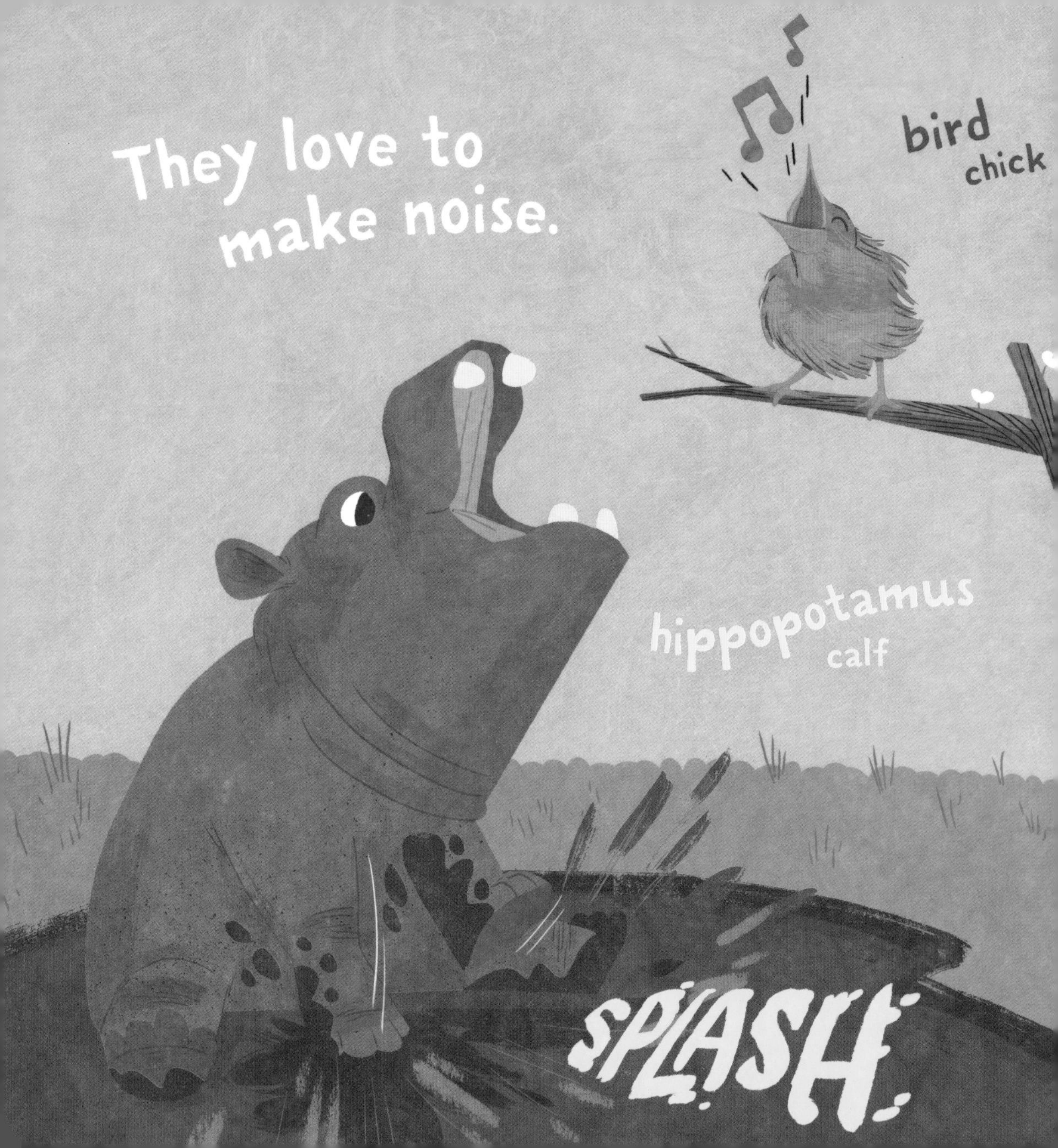

They love to snuggle.

bear
cub

rabbit
kitten

owl
owlet

giraffe
calf

INDESTRUCTIBLES®

BOOKS BABIES CAN REALLY SINK ...INTO!

Baby likes to play in the bath. So does baby elephant!

Baby likes to eat. So do baby monkey and baby chipmunk!

Baby loves to make noise! Just like baby bird,
baby pig, and baby hippo!

Teach baby all about baby animals in a book that's INDESTRUCTIBLE

Dear Parents: INDESTRUCTIBLES are built for the way babies "read": with their hands and mouths. INDESTRUCTIBLES won't rip or tear and are 100% washable. They're made for baby to hold, grab, chew, pull, and bend.

$5.95 U.S.   ISBN 978-0-7611-9308

9 780761 193081   50595

Copyright © 2017 by Indestructibles, Inc. Used under license.
Illustrations copyright © 2017 by Workman Publishing Co., Inc.
Library of Congress Cataloging-in-Publication Data is available.
WORKMAN is a registered trademark of Workman Publishing Co., Inc.
First printing March 2017
10 9 8 7 6 5 4 3 2 1

All INDESTRUCTIBLES books have been safety-tested a
meet or exceed ASTM-F963 and CPSIA guidelin
INDESTRUCTIBLES is a registered trademark of TyBook
Contact specialmarkets@workman.com regard
special discounts for bulk purchas
Printed in Ch

WORKMAN PUBLISHING CO., INC. 225 Varick Street, New York, NY 10014 • workman.com/indestructibles